John Boynton Priestley was born in 1894 in Bradford. At the age of 16 he went into the wool business and began to write his first newspaper columns (for the 'Bradford Pioneer', the weekly journal of Bradford's Labour Party).

Once war broke out Priestley joined the West Riding Regiment in September 1914 as one of Kitchener's 'First 100,000'. He served on the Western Front and in the Battle of Loos, in 1917 he was commissioned as an officer until, in the summer of 1918, injuries sustained in a gas attack led him to be classified as unfit for active service.

J.B. Priestley published his first book in 1922 and
major, and
twentieth-ce
to write play
West End th

GW00537972

still produced around the world. During World War Two Priestley presented the BBC Radio programme Postscript, which drew audiences of up to 16 million, and led Graham Greene to describe Priestley as "a leader second only in importance to Mr Churchill".

In 1957 Priestley was instrumental in the foundation of the Campaign for Nuclear Disarmament (CND). J.B. Priestley died on August 14th 1984.

The Town
Major of
Miraucourt

J. B. PRIESTLEY

TURNPIKE BOOKS

First published in 1930 by Heinemann
This edition published by Turnpike Books 2018

turnpikebooks@gmail.com

ISBN 9780993591334

Typeset by M Rules

Printed in Great Britain by Clays Ltd, St Ives plc

The Town
Major of
Miraucourt

If I am to describe how I found them, I must begin some way off, for they were not, so to speak, round a corner but at the end of a queer road, perhaps a tunnel. To understand the circumstances, you have to appreciate the special quality of a whole period, not a mere hour or two or a day, but weeks, swelling into months. At the end of this period, anything might have happened, and something did. I could throw the thing at you – there, take it or leave it! – but that would not be wise, would not be just, for it had not been suddenly thrown at me without preparation. A lot of things had been thrown at me, had really come out of the blue, before that.

One of them was a gas shell, which had come too near me in the summer of 1918, so that I became a casualty for the third (and, I trust, last) time. From the hospital, where I had listened for days and days and days to the autobiography of a brown little doctor from Arizona, I was forwarded, a wheezy parcel, to the Medical Board Base Depot in Rouen. There were worse places, far worse places, than the M.B.B.D., Rouen. You waited there until the medical board, yawning and in despair, decided to see you, and perhaps after that until it decided, now yawning harder than ever and deeper in despair, to see you again. We officers earned our keep there by censoring vast piles of letters or going to distant huts and paying out hordes of troops who always appeared to come from either the Hebrides or the West Indies; you sat there hour after hour, while some purple quarter-master-sergeant called out the

most outlandish names. The mess was
like a railway refreshment rooms towards
the end of an hysterical Bank Holiday;
even at breakfast time the likeness
was still there; but it had an unlimited
supply of those small export bottles of
Guinness's Stout at one franc the bottle,
and you spent most of your leisure order-
ing more and more of these bottles and
conducting long and idiotic arguments
with men you had never seen before and
never wanted to see again. Towards mid-
night, the infantry and the engineers
began to swear at one another … There
were other amusements. Round the
corner was the best soccer team in the

world, twenty-two International legs too
precious, too beautiful, to be exposed to
red-hot fragments of shell. There was
also a camp music-hall where a whole
series of R.A.M.C. orderlies pretended
to be George Robey or Leslie Henson. It
was not a bad life: the pile of letters, the
heap of franc notes to be paid out, then
back to the bottle-strewn smoky mess,
the stout, and the idiotic arguments; but
it was not quite real. I could not place it
on the map.

The medical board decided that I
was B2, or something like that, and
the M.B.B.D. had no further use for
me. I was told to report at the other

side of the town. There I found a very neat little colonel in a depressing little house in a back street. The house came straight out of realistic French fiction of the later 'Eighties, but the colonel was fighting it – tooth and nailbrush. This explained his responsible air, his solemnity: he was an English gentleman keeping his end up in the remote waste places. He spoke to me gravely about dinner and dress. (Perhaps I could find him, even now, somewhere behind those wire-screened windows in Savile Row, disdainfully turning over the newest range of Gents' fancy suitings.) The depot itself was a large factory building, which swarmed with men who never seemed quite real, unlike the men one knew in the trenches, who had been real people to a hair. There was something ghostly about these fellows, perhaps because they were very tired, very bored. Only the sergeants, spick and span, terrific saluters and callers to attention, were familiar figures. You met them, keeping the old flag flying, the brass buttons polished, at every base; real professional soldiers, waiting for this unwieldy amateur affair, this blood-thirsty melodrama of bombing bank clerks and machine-gunning gardeners, to blow itself to pieces. This factory had been turned into a sort of lunatic labour exchange. You had only to make out, in correct triplicate, the proper indent for any kind of labour, and we would supply it. Entertainers were our favourite commodity. If the Fourth Army wanted two comedians, three conjurors, a couple of female impersonators, and a few baritones, it sent us a wire saying so, and we paraded the most likely specimens, tried one or two on the stage (we had an excellent stage on the third floor), and packed them off by the next train. Fresh relays of comedians and female impersonators arrived every day or so, had their kits and pay-books inspected, their claims to histrionic talent investigated, and were handed over to the beery and brilliantined sergeants. There are times when I do not believe any longer in that fantastic depot, and tell myself that all vague memories of it must be packed up and huddled away with the scenery of old dreams.

During dinner, in the little house, we talked a good deal about the War, which was beginning to wobble. We pointed out to one another that we were winning. There was even talk of a possible armistice, and once or twice we had champagne on the strength of it.

A new arrival came to share my room, a tall thin youth with a slight squint, and he could talk of nothing but Miss Nellie Taylor, the musical comedy actress, whom he had once met in Birmingham. The streets smelled of autumn, and dead leaves drifted down the canal. A smokiness came in the morning and returned early in the evening; the little house was besieged by dank air; and the men were more ghostly than ever as they limped up and down the stairs of the mad factory. I ate and drank heartily, smoked my pipe, sat in the orderly room or inspected kits, sent for conjurors, and talked about the War and Miss

Nellie Taylor; but I did these things mechanically, without inner conviction. I had lost my bearings. I had lost one set at the beginning of September, 1914, when I walked into a dismantled picture palace with a dirty blanket over my arm and tried to sleep on the same floor with about five hundred other recruits and fifty old tramps who had sneaked in for shelter. Perhaps I had never exactly found my bearings during the four years that followed, when every horizon spat and belched and erupted and rockets of death went hooting and flaring every night; but I had come to some sort of terms with the shattering idiocy, like a man sharing a house, year after year, with a lunatic. Nothing that had happened before, however, neither in the mysterious golden war before August, 1914, nor in the War itself, had prepared me for these antics in Rouen. And there was perhaps always a suspicion in one's mind that the whole thing might be slipping out of any kind of control, even that of roaring death. Sanity, one concluded, might easily be bombed away for good and all, and the portion of this world from now on might be fantasy with broad interludes of slapstick. Already, perhaps, generals were beginning to whiten their cheeks and put vermilion on their noses, and there were telephone inquiries to the docks at Havre about the first consignments of paper hoops. When I was off duty, wandering down the side-streets or by the darkening canal, I was faintly plagued by such suspicions. On duty, there was no time: I was in the ring with the rest, waiting for my turn to be rolled in the carpet and poulticed with custard pies.

There came a morning when the adjutant took me aside after breakfast. This adjutant was an enormous, plump, pink fellow, who wore most unconvincing curly little bits of ginger whisker and moustache. He had a passion for gramophone records, and nothing written by Mr. Nat D. Ayer escaped him or us. He was unreal even then, in that atmosphere. Consider, then, the fright I had, earlier this very year of 1929, when an enormous, plump, pink creature, with wildly unconvincing curly little bits of ginger whisker and moustache, passed me, not once but three times, in the stalls of a theatre. I stared and stared, merely puzzled at first but soon quite startled. It was he. Somehow he had contrived to push himself through into this world of rates and taxes and depositions. It was not simply as if I had seen a ghost, but as if I had once been a ghost and had suddenly recognised an old spectral neighbour. He did not see me, and I did not speak to him. Something might have happened if I had spoken to him – a roll of thunder somewhere, perhaps a flash and then nothing left in the aisle of the stalls but a gigantic suit of dress-clothes, quivering and smoking a little. But on that old morning of legend, he took me aside and suggested that I might like to see an unusually large draft of men to its destination at a Corps headquarters. This is how I came to discover Miraucourt.

The men were not going there. Nobody was going there. The destination of the draft was a very different place, and there is no reason why I should mention its name. In the middle of the afternoon we boarded a train at Rouen, and this train, after innumerable whistles and groans and wheezings, pulled out and ran nearly half a mile, after which it stopped for four hours, and then returned, with many a whimsical shrug, to a siding at Rouen, where its engine was used as a hot-water urn for tea by the men. After that, for two days, I sat in my windowless compartment and stared at the autumn, which was moving nearly as fast as we were. When the train could do no more for us, we climbed into some lorries and went rattling down roads given over to dust and Chinese coolies. We limped up to Corps Headquarters, and my duty was done. I did not linger there. I had to get back to Rouen, and I was determined to try a different route, for otherwise I might find myself on that train again. Nobody at Corps Headquarters cared what I did: they did not know what they were doing themselves. So I claimed a seat in a lorry that appeared to be going more or less in the right direction, and, after a few more hours of dust and Chinese coolies, it landed me in a little valley composed of two chalky hillsides, vast mounds of props and rusted barbed wire, and an ancient Irish Colonel who was living in the smallest and chalkiest Nissen hut I have ever seen. He appeared to have been there for a long time, and may have been left over from some other war. We crouched in the hut, like two leprechauns, and he gave me some warm Maconochie and Jameson and chalky water in an aluminium cap, and then we sat at the door, under the mild stars, and he pulled his long drooping moustache and crooned at me. His subject was fly-fishing. Somewhere behind us, beyond those mild stars it seemed, the air thudded.

The lorry I boarded next morning – I suppose it carried the colonel's Maconochie and Jameson – was not going to Miraucourt. Nobody, nothing, I repeat, was going there. I had never heard of it then, and I have never heard of it since. Miraucourt was never mentioned. This lorry was bound for Custincourt, but I never arrived there. A dashing corporal on a motor-cycle stopped us, produced his orders, and the lorry had to turn around. It was wanted elsewhere, and not the way I wanted to go, so there was nothing for it but to get out and – as they liked to say in those days – proceed independently. The corporal, who had arrived out of the blue, returned there. The lorry driver and his mate had no suggestions to offer; they know the road to Custincourt, and that was all; and they did not advise me to try it on foot. While I was still hesitating, there came a wreck of a cart on which were perched a bearded peasant and one of those little French boys who are all bones and eyes. Their destination was the hamlet, the mere speck, of Bovincourt – not any Bovincourt you ever knew – and they would take me there, for beyond Bovincourt, a few kilometres, was a great village, a town one might say, a considerable place, where there were soldiers English and an officer of the first importance, as all the world knew, since this long time. In this fashion then, among the jolting potatoes, I came to Bovincourt, where they pointed out the track that would lead me to the great village and the officer of the first importance. It was called Miraucourt. Clearly, the officer was a Town Major. So down the narrow lane I went, to report myself to the Town Major of Miraucourt.

They had, as usual, under-estimated the distance, and that track went spinning out kilometres long after it

ought to have stopped. I only passed
two people on the way. The first was
an old woman who gave my uniform
a surly look, I thought, and mumbled
something unpleasant as I went by.
The second was a cheerful slut of a girl,
driving two cows, a girl who seemed
almost too favourably disposed towards
my uniform, for she giggled and made
round eyes at it. I gathered from these
two encounters that the English at
Miraucourt were on certain terms
with their hostesses, living in a mixed
atmosphere of approval and disapproval.
Then I arrived, dusty, a little footsore,
and parched, at the village itself, which

showed me its red roofs among the plane trees just as I had decided that it could not possibly exist. It was one of those villages and little towns that are hidden from you until the last moment, when they spring out, like a waggish uncle, and give you a pleasant surprise. The War had not touched it. Not a tile was missing. It was built snugly about a square, and had an air of cosiness you rarely find in France. A few women and old men were hanging about, but there were no signs of the military, not a single glimpse of khaki. The long shadows of late afternoon were creeping across the square, and all the noises of the world were crumbling away. Somewhere, beyond the darkening bosom of those hills, there was a war, but it seemed incredibly remote, the wildest rumour of violence and sudden death.

The first thing I had to do was to find the Town Major's office, and that did not take me long. I found it on the ground floor of a fat little house in the square. The door was open, so I marched in. That absurd office ought to have given me the first hint of what was happening to me, but I do not think it did. The room was an incredible jumble of bottles of every size and shape, mostly empty, cigar and cheroot boxes, broken gramophone records, dubious literature, and the more opulent illustrations from *La Vie Parisienne* and similar periodicals. There were military papers there too, of course, stacks of them, but they were lying about in a hopeless confusion, and many of them seemed to have been torn across, presumably to make spills. Hanging behind a door was the most voluminous officer's tunic I have ever seen, a major's, and decorated with a number of mysterious medal ribbons. Evidently the Town Major of Miraucourt was an enormous fellow. Facing the table was a very large arm-chair that was leaning, as if in despair, to one side, where its hind leg was propped up with two or three volumes of official regulations. And on the table, flung down carelessly upon the litter of bottles and papers, was a gigantic Sam Browne belt, monstrous in its girth. But there was no sign of the major himself nor of any orderly or batman. Nothing stirred but a reek of onions.

I was by this time badly in need of food and drink, so I crossed the square to the *Estaminet* of the Little Calf. The proprietress was a very different creature from the usual sallow and harassed vendor of fried eggs and grenadine. She was a ripe and bustling female, blue-eyed and moist. She seemed glad to see me but rather surprised, as if stray English officers were a rarity. When I told her I could not find the Town Major, she stuck out her lower lip, wagged her head drolly, then laughed, as if the very thought of him was entertaining. He had, it seemed, his affairs, and would doubtless return before the night, though he did not always so return, oh no. Meanwhile, I could have something to eat, something to drink. She left me sitting by the window, with a silent, pipe-sucking old peasant for company. And then I saw two figures in khaki crossing the square.

When they drew nearer, I could see they were a couple of hard-bitten corporals. They had that curious wooden swagger of the "old sweat." One of them was distinguished by a great beak of nose, so red, so inflamed, that it was a conflagration in flesh. The other had one of those flat, almost pushed-in faces: he was the kind of man who always talks out of a corner of his mouth, as if everything he has to say is a bitter secret. They were both wearing an incredible number of wound stripes and blue chevrons. Just before they reached the door of the *estaminet*, the flat-faced one halted: the other pulled up too; and their voices reached me through the open window.

"'E'll give me something, an' 'andy, too," the flat-faced one was saying. "That's my ruddy style. 'E gets me my leaf or 'e gives me the eighty francs 'e's dropped on the mudhook, one or the other. An' I'll tell 'im so, sergeant-major or no flamin' sergeant-major. I'll give 'im the office. That's my ruddy style."

"Take it easy, chum, take it easy," replied the other, the one with the nose. "You'll get it in time. You'll get it."

"I want it now, an' I'll get it or I'll know the flamin' reason. That's my ruddy style."

"Where's the queer feller gone this afternoon?"

"Ask me! Promenad avec vous with Mar-ee, that'll be 'is ticket."

"No, 'e isn't. Saw 'er meself a bit back. 'E must be lookin' over the rookies."

"'E can start lookin' for my eighty francs. All right then. Lead on for the pig's ear. That's my ruddy style."

The next moment, they were inside, gaping at me. They were even more surprised to see a strange officer than the proprietress was. Evidently very few people found their way to Miraucourt. This did not astonish me. I do not think anything would have astonished me. That was the way things were going.

They saluted smartly enough, but then promptly retired before I had a chance to say anything to them. "Cor lumme!" I heard one of them cry, and then the other one began, "'Ere," in what seemed to be an aggrieved tone, as if I had no right to be there. But then, I do not know if I had any right to be there.

Madame returned, a trifle flustered, with some soup and bread, and said that if I went back there, later in the evening, I could have an *entrecote*, some salad, some fruit, a little bottle of wine, in short, quite a dinner. Meanwhile, this snack would ease the pangs. After the soup and bread, perhaps a little drink, to give me comfort? She had the excellent liqueur of Martinique, perhaps I would try that? I rather weakly assented, and actually had three glasses of the dark and mysterious spirit. That was not very much, but it was enough to blur the fine edges of sight and hearing, to conjure forth the oddest fancies and give them the colour of reality, to introduce that fatal subjective element into things. There was something very curious about that liqueur of Martinique. But it suited Miraucourt. It might have been distilled for the place. Perhaps it was.

Nevertheless, I am sure that I saw and heard the sergeant-major and his little squad in the square outside. They came before daylight had faded and while all was quiet. Oh, they were there all right! There were six of them in the squad, and even in the motley army of the last desperate year, in the flotsam and jetsam of soldiery I had noticed in the labour depot at Rouen, I had never seen half a dozen such awkward and forlorn creatures gathered together on parade. They all appeared to be wearing one another's uniforms; they were not the right shape; they were all heads, feet, elbows, and hands; they were anything but soldiers. This could not be said of the sergeant-major, who was soldierly enough, too soldierly, in fact, in the antique style. He was a thinnish fellow, who strutted and pranced in the absurdest fashion. I could not see his face very clearly, but it was a purplish hue and was decorated with one of those long waxed moustaches that brought little tubes of Hungarian Pomade into the barbers' shops of yesterday. Like the corporals, he was wearing ribbons, gold stripes, and chevrons enough to suggest that he had been soldiering not merely since this Mons but the Mons before that, had been swaggering on and

off parade, mostly off, since the Fifth
Harry's time.

He brought his six misfits quite close
to the *estaminet* and then, with a fear-
ful bellow, halted them. I went to the
door. Evidently their movements had
displeased him, as well they might.
He set them going again, like rusted
clockwork figures, and then went
through the whole repertoire of familiar
barrack-square jeers. "Yer might break
yer mother's 'eart but yer won't break
mine – *Errboutt Turrn!*" and "Don't
forget while you tea's getting colder,
mine's getting 'otter, an' I can stay
'ere all day." There were others too,

about wooden soldiers; in fact, all the old jibes. When he had brought them back again, one of them must have protested, said that he was sick or something of that kind, for immediately this sergeant-major plunged into the most fantastic and passionate speech.

"What, you bag of rotten dumplings, you flea-bitten turnip-eater!" he roared. "Are we soldiers or are we bloody scarecrows? Are there no Huns to fight? Do King and Country call? Is Belgium Kaiser Bill's? Who's for the peg? Speak up, you Derby rats!"

"Please, zur," quavered one of them.

"Silence, you suet," he continued,

working himself up into an astonishing rage. "God let me live, are we conchies? Do we object while Empire falls? Has Hindenburg the laugh? Soldiers yet, if we 'ave to skin you! The 'eathen in his blindness bows down to wood an' stone. Two-an'-thirty sergeants an' corporals forty-one. You put some *juldee* in it, or I'll *marrow* you this minute. Are we not White Men? Mons, Wipers, Nerve Chapelle, Vimy, an' Martinpush, that's me, an' before yer number was dry. Women an' children first an' keep the old flag flying. *Dis-miss.*" And he turned away, purple, magnificent, leaving the six gaping and scratching their heads. I will swear that is exactly what I saw and heard, Martinique or no Martinique.

Moreover, before I could return to my chair, I saw the Town Major himself. He was crossing the square at the other side, going towards his office, an enormous fellow, quite old but still fairly sprightly, and he was wearing the twin of that tunic I had seen hanging behind the door, and a colossal pair of slacks. He moved across that square like a brown galleon with the fires of sunset in his topsails. And behind him, trying to catch him up, was the giggling damsel I had passed in the lane, a little cleaner now, better dressed, and carrying a basket. He disappeared into the little villa, unaware of her. She followed him, and, after a moment's hesitation I slipped across the square and followed her. I waited a few minutes, then knocked at his office door, through which was coming the sound of tittering expostulations in the *patois* of the neighbourhood. A sonorous voice told me to go away: I saw no sound military reason why I should go away, so I knocked again. This time the door was flung open. I was confronted by the major, whose vast bulk quite obscured the girl behind him.

"What's this?" he cried. "A soldier? Will they never end, these wars?"

I reported myself to him, as solemnly as I could. He was old and amazingly fat, immense, ruinous, and unbuttoned, but his eyes, creased round though they were until sometimes they nearly disappeared altogether, blazed with intelligence and humour. I can see them shining yet through the mist of inter-vening years and the time's lunacies and the fumes of Martinique.

"Come in," he cried, and stepped back, at the same time looking with a droll assumption of surprise and severity at the girl, who seemed to be removing certain traces of disorder. He waved a hand at her and then dismissed her in fluent but queer French, telling her to be a little earlier next time and to find larger eggs and fatter chickens. "A good girl," he remarked when she had gone, "but the child of dishonest parents. They bleed us, these French peasants. They take advantage of our innocence. We are anybody's mark, we old soldiers. We go away to the wars and whether we are ever seen again, nobody cares, as somebody said to me years ago, before your time. Here I am – who might have had a brigade – Town Major of a place so small there's not a man can go on leave for fear he'll never find it again. I shall take it home with me as a keepsake. I've a sergeant-major who can't write, two corporals who can't read, and now six men who can't walk. But they can all eat and drink. And we're so far away from anybody, they won't send us proper rations. What we get now is what there happens to be a glut of. The week before last, nothing arrived here but a load of socks and puttees, not a tin of anything you could eat. Last week, it was worse; they sent up a load of wire and sandbags, devil a thing else. I've had sun-helmets, diving-boots, sailors' hammocks, and tins of paint for armoured cars in desert warfare, all dumped on me in place of ration issue. We're expecting half an observation balloon next or seven gross of snow spectacles, or five carrier-pigeon outfits, without the pigeons, for fear we should be remembering the taste of food in our mouths and be eating them. And what with that and the press of business," he added, pouring himself out a drink, then pushing the bottle towards me, "I'm so villainous low, I've half a mind to take up drinking and looking at the women, and let the war rot. Fill up, my lad, don't stint it. Madame across the way there's got another bottle of the same handy, and it won't take you a minute to slip out and get it when we've finished this. And what do you want me to do for you?"

I explained where I was going, where I had been, and all about it, to all of which he paid very little attention. He had now lit a cheroot, and was sprawling monstrously at his ease, in his lop-sided arm-chair.

"There's a bunk and a blanket or two you can have to-night up there," and he jerked a thumb at the ceiling. "Tell one of the corporals or the sergeant-major, any of them. Just call 'Smith' when you're going out. It's the damnedest and oddest thing in the world, but we're all Smiths here, every man jack of us. I'm Major F. Smith. There's Sergeant-major P. Smith. There's two Corporal Smiths, B. Smith and N. Smith."

I had hardly time to digest this – though indeed I never did digest it because I never succeeded in swallowing it – before there came a knock at the door and there entered two elderly little Frenchmen, dressed neatly in black and obviously two local officials. They were furiously angry and began pouring out a torrent of remonstrance even at the very threshold. This and that, it seemed, were abominable, and could not be endured another day, another hour, another moment.

The major rose from his chair and patted them each on the shoulder. Then he turned to me. "If I don't fetch off these two little black shavings of Monseers, there'll be no peace for the British Army, and this one on my right will scream himself into hysterics. He's lathering now, and smells of goat. Go find your bunk, my boy, and make it early to bed. Leave it to us old soldiers, we're hard wearing. Kitchener never meant to use you so hard. He told me himself. I knew him well. Go to Madame of the Little Calf – though

she's not that, either – and tell her
from me to treat you well; give her fifty
francs for me; eat a little, take water
with your wine, write to your mother,
your sister, say your prayers, and then
sleep sound."

It was the corporal with the great
red nose who showed me my bunk and
found some blankets for me. We hardly
exchanged a word because we were
both too busy listening to the other
corporal and the sergeant-major who,
in defiance of all military discipline,
were quarrelling furiously and at the
top of their voices: I do not know where
they were, but I could hear them plainly

enough. "That's my ruddy style," the flat-faced kept shouting, over and over again; while the sergeant-major, in his turn, retorted wildly with "Base cur," and "Filthy mudhook wrangler," and other, more fantastic terms. This did not astonish me. It is hard to say exactly now, but I think that by this time I had guessed who they all were. The corporal and his nose vanished; I descended the shadowy stairs; and as I passed the major's door, I heard no voices raised in anger but roars of laughter, which followed me out into the square. I knew that by this time he was sitting at ease with the two little officials, who would not remember their grievances, which I had no doubt were real enough, until they left that room and his tropical presence.

The dinner that Madame had promised was ready, and I lingered over it, dreamily finishing the wine. A few old men drifted in and out, but I saw none of the English, not a glimpse of the two corporals, the sergeant-major, and the great major himself. Twice, however, Madame, very buxom, very gay, hurried through, carrying a smoking tray and a bottle or two, and I knew she was taking it all across to the major. Nor did she return in a hurry. She was there, though, to tell me what I owed her, to bid me good night, and tell me I was a brave boy. When I turned out at last into the square, now a pool of purple with sable banks and a faintly spangled canopy above, the little house across the way was dark, and, though I was sleepy now and hazy with dream, I did not return there but wandered with my pipe among the shadows of the village. It must have been an hour later when I came back, saw that the major's window was bright gold in the dark, and crept up to it.

Yes, they were there, major and men together, toping it in unbuttoned ease

while the seven stars paled, as they had
so often done before. They had not
changed to the sight; the moustachios,
the cut of the hair, the uniforms and
badges were ours; but now they had
dropped all pretence of being contem-
poraries of men, mortal men, and I
caught the old rich phrases, dripping
with sherris-sack, rolling out into the
night while they bickered and jested
and roared. And now I knew I could
not join them, that if I opened the
door, or even merely tapped on the
window, some magic would be broken;
they would be huddled back into Smiths
again, the Smiths I might find round

any corner; or perhaps they would not be there at all. So I did nothing but stare, out of the dark, until at last I felt too cold, too sleepy, too hazy, to stand there any longer, and tiptoed past the door, up the stairs, to my blankets.

The sergeant I saw next morning was a good fellow, who understood the art of lorry-jumping, knew the roads, and was at some pains to show me exactly how I could find my way from Miraucourt back to Rouen. He was a talkative soul too, and explained how he came to be there and why he had been absent the day before. I could have asked him anything in reason. But I could not ask him what had become of Falstaff, Pistol, Bardolph, and Nym, not even when I was in the act of boarding the lorry, because that would not have seemed to him in reason. He was obviously a man who knew where to draw a line, even in 1918. I have always found that difficult at all times, and then it was impossible. I returned to the factory at Rouen, to find the stairs more ghostly than ever with dim men, conjurors in brisk demand, the little colonel more exquisitely turned out, the curly red adjutant still sweating over the gramophone handle, and talk of Peace added to the talk of War and Miss Nellie Taylor. And if I had started drawing lines, I might have had to draw one clean through the middle of that factory, through Rouen itself, and then where would we be?

Why, we should never know.